W9-AVS-858

This igloo book belongs to:

....

igloobooks

Illustrated by Marina Le Ray

Copyright © 2017 Igloo Books Ltd

An imprint of Igloo Books Group,
part of Bonnier Books UK
bonnierbooks.co.uk

Published in 2020
by Igloo Books Ltd, Cottage Farm
Sywell, NN6 0BJ
All rights reserved, including the right of reproduction
in whole or in part in any form.

Manufactured in China. 0620 002
10 9 8 7 6 5 4 3

Library of Congress Cataloging-in-Publication
Data is available upon request.

ISBN 978-1-78810-075-5
IglooBooks.com
bonnierbooks.co.uk

The Wheels on the Bus

igloobooks

The wheels on the bus go round and round,
round and round, round and round.
The wheels on the bus go round and round, all through the town.

The animals on the bus get on and off, on and off, on and off.
The animals on the bus get on and off, all through the town.

The money on the bus goes jingle-jangle-jingle,
jingle-jangle-jingle, jingle-jangle-jingle.
The money on the bus goes jingle-jangle-jingle, all through the town.

The driver on the bus goes, "Move on back,
move on back, move on back."
The driver on the bus goes, "Move on back," all through the town.

The bell on the bus goes ding-ding-ding,
ding-ding-ding, ding-ding-ding.
The bell on the bus goes ding-ding-ding, all through the town.

The monkeys on the bus go oo-oo-oo, oo-oo-oo, oo-oo-oo.
The monkeys on the bus go oo-oo-oo, all through the town.

The motor on the bus goes vroom-vroom-vroom,
vroom-vroom-vroom, vroom-vroom-vroom.
The motor on the bus goes vroom-vroom-vroom, all through the town.

The horn on the bus goes beep-beep-beep,
beep-beep-beep, beep-beep-beep.
The horn on the bus goes beep-beep-beep, all through the town.

The mother hippos on the bus go chatter-chatter-chatter,
chatter-chatter-chatter, chatter-chatter-chatter.
The mother hippos on the bus go chatter-chatter-chatter,
all through the town.

The daddy elephants on the bus go nod-nod-nod,
nod-nod-nod, nod-nod-nod.
The daddy elephants on the bus go nod-nod-nod,
all through the town.

The wipers on the bus go swish-swish-swish,
swish-swish-swish, swish-swish-swish.
The wipers on the bus go swish-swish-swish, all through the town.

The puddles on the road go splash-splash-splash,
splash-splash-splash, splash-splash-splash.
The puddles on the road go splash-splash-splash, all through the town.

The baby lions on the bus go, "Wah-wah-wah,
wah-wah-wah, wah-wah-wah."
The baby lions on the bus go, "Wah-wah-wah,"
all through the town.

The tiger tots on the bus go giggle-giggle-giggle,
giggle-giggle-giggle, giggle-giggle-giggle.
The tiger tots on the bus go giggle-giggle-giggle,
all through the town.

The traffic lights outside go stop, wait, go,
stop, wait, go, stop, wait, go.
The traffic lights outside go stop, wait, go,
all through the town.

The signals on the bus go blink-blink-blink,
blink-blink-blink, blink-blink-blink.
The signals on the bus go blink-blink-blink,
all through the town.

The grandpa gorillas on the bus go snore-snore-snore,
snore-snore-snore, snore-snore-snore.
The grandpa gorillas on the bus go snore-snore-snore,
all through the town.

The grandma crocodiles on the bus go, "Shh-shh-shh, shh-shh-shh, shh-shh-shh."
The grandma crocodiles on the bus go, "Shh-shh-shh," all through the town.

The bus goes around town until the sun goes down,
the sun goes down, the sun goes down.
The bus goes around town until the sun goes down, all through the town.

The animals on the bus go, "Here's my stop!
Here's my stop! Here's my stop!"
The animals on the bus go, "Here's my stop!" all through the town.

All through the town.